The Light
on Faraway Hill

And Other Stories By,

~J.R. Packard~

CONTENTS

THE GAME OF RECALLING HISTORY

CHAPTER ONE

"DOES ANYONE KNOW WHAT happened two-thousand years ago?" The teacher asked the class.

"That was the year of subjugation." A girl mouse responded. "It was a time when rats ruled and mice followed; when liberties favored those of a larger size."

"That's right. We remember history so we do not forget who is to forever be blamed. The rats once had their days, and now the time of mice reign. Never forget who is to blame, class. If we forget history we are doomed to repeat it. We are doomed at the hands of rats."

I, a rat humbly named George, sat quietly at my desk clenching my fists in anger. Angry that I was in the midst of a people so hateful at someone innocent of ever having committed an atrocity. That I was scorned for something my forefathers did. It wasn't always like that, and it certainly wasn't in the present year of 2052: the year of Anti-rat-ism. Mice and rats once got along in harmony, long before anyone's time. I know it for what it was. I read the old books. Sixteenth, seventeenth, and eighteenth B.C. century literature. Books now outlawed for their archaic ways. Their words of old traditions and old truths are now held in contempt as dogmatic and overbearing. The dogma of today is *change*, in any way one may imagine it. But now it's different and days of rat control have long passed.

Indeed, I sit midsummer at my desk in the old abandoned lighthouse, surrounded by children of the times. We are mixed up and lost in the convoluted world that we have fashioned. Like spiders who have laid their eggs in the midst of winter, knowing not that their children will perish because of it.

As it was told, rats once believed themselves to be higher than mice. They believed, because of their size and physical capabilities, that they were more noble than the meek mouse. It was a dark time, but no less dim than mine. The mouse is more susceptible to predators; weaker scavengers; less clever. Perhaps these were the greatest justifications for the disparities.

"And what prevents the rat from overtaking the mouse again?" Asked another student.

"Control." Answered the teacher. "It is our due control to make sure rats cannot speak against mice any longer. It is a crime against the species of mice and cannot be tolerated. If you notice any amount of Anti-mice-ism, it is your duty to suppress their speech and prevent them from having a platform."

"But what if that rat manages to have a voice and evades Anti-mice speech? What if he accepts the backlash?" Asked the student.

"Everything must be done to tarnish their reputation." The teacher continued. "Unfortunately, as it is, it remains legal for a rat to speak unjustly. It is, however, illegal for a rat to write/publish or run any business with Anti-mice sentiment surrounding it. The best course of action is, in a sense, to allow them mildly to speak their opinion. If such is done correctly, and without great repercussions, it gives the rat an ego-boost, which in turn will entice them to perform an illegal act, which can then be punished under law therewith. Therefore, go after the rat. If this tactic fails, lay off of them for a week. Let them grow their voice, just enough to the point where they slip up. Then pounce."

The bell suddenly rang. I began my way out of the room until a mouse "accidentally" knocked one of my textbooks out of my hands. I quietly picked it up and dared not to say a word. The school day ended thereafter and I made my way down the halls until I saw Rachel. She, a fellow rat, had been my closest friend since we were children, and I trusted her more than any in the school. I walked to her while she opened her locker.

"I have a surprise for you." She said.

"What is it?"

She then uncovered a cloth wrapping hidden far into the locker, revealing an old book. It read "Huckleberry Finn".

"Where did you get that?" I exclaimed. "I've never heard of it, but surely it is illegal. I can tell by the cover's old style."

"I bargained for it with a dealer last night." She replied. "It cost me a fair bit of money, but it was worth it."

"Have you read it?" I asked.

"Just the first few sentences. I wanted to do it with you."

Rachel was a girl who never quite followed the rules. Not quite a delinquent and yet far from the typical prep-schooler. I always prided her on the fact of her toughness. Where I would generally coward and keep my thoughts to myself, she would never relent to adversity. Still, she was always the kindest girl one could meet, and had a smile that could light a whole room.

"We'll meet at my house in an hour. That will give us privacy while my parents are away at work."

I agreed.

Shortly thereafter I made my way to her house after walking down the ragged streets. She had a nicer home than most, and I always enjoyed going there. We went into her room, locked the door, and began to open the book.

"Who's Mark Twain?" She asked.

"I've heard of him in various other works, but have never read any of his stuff." I replied.

We read through, eventually realizing what in fact we were reading. The first few paragraphs alone were filled to the brim with illegal words and phrases. Truly, if we were caught, we'd be fined at least, or jailed at the worst for hate crimes. In the eye's of the Ninth Society (our leaders), we could have been the ones who had written the book ourselves. There would be no way to prove it otherwise. Indeed, the words were more than beautiful; they were enlightening. It was refreshing to read works so elegant in words; those free of propaganda and political agendas. I knew not whether this "Mark Twain" was a mouse or a rat, and I did not care in the slightest. Yes, I always believed that both rats and mice had the potential to make the most delightful art. We continued rushing through the pages the rest of the night. Analyzing every page, word for word, and enjoying the escape which it provided.

THE DOCTRINE OF ALTERATION
CHAPTER TWO

THE FOLLOWING DAY, I left my parents to return again to my twelfth grade English class. This day was different, however. The teacher looked more serious than she had yesterday. She set upon each desk a new assigned book for us to read. It was in all white. Blank in every sense of the word, save for four bold, black words on the front of it reading: "A Commentary On Alteration". I knew immediately what the book was about. "Alteration", as it were, was the religion of my society. I read in my old books about Christianity and Islamism, but as for the doctrine of the lighthouse, Alteration was the dogma.

"I would like everyone to read this book in one week's time. We will then have a test on the matter, and those who fail will be required to attend a meeting with the head staff." The teacher explained.

I knew what the book was about before I would even consider reading it. Alteration is an Anti-rat ideology, though it masquerades itself as a "progressive and moral" idea. In truth, it is nothing more than the most heinous of notions. I was always a man of tradition. One of keeping working things the way they were. Now that is not to say I didn't believe in change. Were it two-thousand or so years ago, I would indeed back the idea of raising mice from the rule of rats. They were in a time of unjustified hardship, and I would've done my diligence to assist them; not meanwhile making them higher than rats however, mind you.

Alteration is the concept of change; to alter anything and everything that should, in the eyes of mice and our government, be changed to fit their narrative. Should a rat have anything more than a mouse, whether it be a larger house, more food, or more income, Alteration dictates that the system should be changed in order for everyone to be "equal", as the Ninth Society would say. In truth, the goal would be to raise up any mice perceived as lower, and then encourage giving more to them. Since they had been subjugated two-thousand years ago, the idea was sort "giving back" or "seeking long-awaited revenge"—though no mouse or rat alive had ever lived through it.

Mice followed the way of Mice-ism, and most rats followed Rat-ism. Rat-ism, by definition, is allowing both rats and mice to do, buy, and sell as they please. In fear that this freedom would allow rats to rise up again, Mice-ism is an anti-freedom creation which masqueraded itself as "protecting the common good". Thus buying and selling should be in the hands of people who can regulate and evenly distribute it: the government. Where Rat-ism allows potential for inequality at the price of opportunity, Mice-ism seeks to destroy opportunity at the price of having everything the same across the board. The Rat-ist sees beauty in the fact that a poor man has the potential to become the richest, and believes if the person works hard enough, he can accomplish such. Meanwhile, the Mice-ist would raise the poor man, whether he does work or not, at the cost of stealing money from those who work the hardest–the rich. They would then call this system equitable, when it seems less than fair, and rather more *equal*. And yet, the mice did not truly believe in equality. What is equal, is giving everyone the same opportunities to become equal. Tyranny is to make the mouse a rat by tearing away his identity as an individual mouse. A rat will never be a mouse, no matter how either one tries. It is nature's inequality, and the solution is to utilize and combine their individual strengths. Forcing a rat to become like a mouse is like forcing a teacup to be tea. It will never work. Separate they have a function, but together they have something new: a proper drink.

Those in my society who force this religion, were called the Ninth Society. They were a group of nine leaders who composed the government. When in the final days of rat rule, the mice instigated a coup, and they put nine of their leaders in charge. Since then, when one dies, another is put in their place. Never exceeding nor decreasing nine. These are our gods; *dictators of decision*. They control who gets what, what gets seen, and what one hears. They were the kings of mice, and self-proclaimed numens of rats. My god lived within myself, and I put no value in their divisive ways. There was no hierarchy in the Society. Like their dogma, all were equal in terms of reach and power. Each one had exceedingly convoluted names; ones I can't even pronounce. Though equal, I do think this was a consequence of their egos. Having an obscure name brings more attention to oneself and makes them stand out more than the rest. Ironic, as they were supposedly indistinguishable.

"Why was the Ninth Society formed?" The teacher asked.

I mustered up the courage to raise my hand. Answering in a way that corresponded to my real readings.

"To suppress the words of rats." I said.

"Wrong." She replied. "We encourage the voices of rats, so long as they do not voice Anti-Mice-ism. That is of course not okay."

"And who dictates what is okay?" I replied in an irritated manner. Was she god? Who was she to proclaim what is morally correct?

"Excuse me?" She replied.

I knew I was stepping far over the line. Indeed, I could press her over something, but she would never give me the consideration of questioning me. I knew for certain consequences would come. I braced for impact.

"Would you like a moral meeting with the staff?"

"No." I responded.

"Then you would do best to not answer."

I kept my mouth shut tightly from then onwards. Perhaps it was my temper getting the best of me, or the fact that I needed to voice the words of verity. In any case, I shouldn't have done it. It put me on the school's radar.

As that was the last class of the day, I went home shortly thereafter. I lived in a lower-class shack, and generally ate meager scraps of thrown out food, but I was content. Though poor, I appreciated the rich. They provided the jobs in society. Seeing as I had not one yet, I felt no entitlement to live in such a grand house as they. I turned on the television and saw on the news that a mouse had been killed in my neighborhood and that the suspect was presumed to be a rat, yet having no evidence to support such a claim. I thought nothing of it, and went to bed shortly afterwards, throwing away the *"Commentary On Alteration"* beforehand.

THE ULTIMATE EVIL
CHAPTER THREE

SCHOOL CONTINUED OFF for three further days, until the weekend came, and I at last had a chance to relax. The day before my break, I had failed my test on Alteration, and was forced into a conduct meeting with the leading staff. I made the excuse that I simply had too much homework to read the book. Needless to say, they were not sympathetic, and I was honored with detention for five days and an essay on why Anti-Mice-ism is against rodent-kind. To write it, was of course the last thing I wanted to do, but I had no choice. To not do so would first likely result in suspension, and if I continued to be tardy on the matter (or refused), I would almost certainly be expelled.

In my society, expulsion did not exist. If it happened, I would not simply be able to be "home-schooled" or have the chance to find another. Instead, I would likely be sent to a re-education camp, where I would have no choice but to disagree. Explosion was not an option. I began writing the essay while I turned the television on to see the update on the recent mouse murder. My brother sat beside me, glued to the screen as though in an obsessed daze that media brings forth in the lighthouse. The news was on for a few minutes before it was abruptly cut off by a Ninth Society broadcast. The nine of them were standing at the podium, dressed in fine gold silk, and wearing elaborate headdresses. In front of them, and set on the podium, was what appeared to be a baby owl. It surprised me, as owls tend to eat mice, but I knew there was a reason behind it. I watched and listened. One of the mice stepped up and said:

"My fellow rodents, we have brought before you the new face of our party. We have found him in the wild, and he has promised us to side with mice and help raise them up. He will aid in our goal of amplifying their voices and becoming a spokesperson for our honorable and venerable Society. Praise be unto the lighthouse of rodents."

Having never seen an owl, I was quite surprised they had found him, and for what purpose was beyond me. They left the reason for napping him up vague, but I saw through it and knew there was some hidden, secondary agenda. Perhaps it was a show of power. Indeed, how could such weaklings as mice garner the side of a powerful being as an owl? They continued:

"After careful consideration, we have decided to construct a very large castle in the heart of the lighthouse. We shall properly call it "The Castle of Alteration". We shall set our face upon its crown, and keep it as a symbol of our reach and might. Furthermore, we have new dictations to pronounce. From now on, private institutions shall hand over sixty percent of their profits over to the hands of our rightly-guided and moral Society. We shall distribute such income evenly across the rodents, while giving priority to mice of lower income than rats therewith. Therefore, fear not fellow mice, we shall have a great influence on the affairs of rat-privilege, and shall make it so you must 'give back what you took' for the atrocities committed thousands of years ago. We ask that you give us more "privileges" in return. Let us help you by helping us. We have your interests in mind, and will not allow 'certain rats' to get ahead while so many mice are left behind. This concludes our message."

I saw then the crowd around them cheer with great exuberance at their words of eminence and personage. I thought little of the matter and the owl at the time, but three weeks later the situation changed. The Castle of Alteration was completely built and the once-small owl had grown to his full adult size. The castle was five feet tall and painted fully black. It had only one gate at its front made entirely in iron, for which only Ninth Society members and Owl were permitted to pass.

It was near that time that a new law was passed. Anytime a law was approved in the lighthouse, an outline of it would be posted on the front doors of all houses. I was to make my way back home from seeing Rachel one day to find a pamphlet. It read:

"To all citizens,

After due consideration, Owl and our most venerable Society has decided that newborn rodents may be killed. This is in the interest of freedom for the people. Babies can be a hardship and obstruction for their 'breeders', therefore let us move forward from the past and 'alter' what requires change so that our town may progress towards a new era of freedom. We will provide peace from the toil of children and they who have the potential to rebel against our holy religion. We especially encourage this removal for rats, who have historically been natural oppressors. Amplify the voices of mice, and let not the rat get the better of us.

In your interests,

The Ninth Society"

I was appalled that innocent children could be barbarically lawfully killed or savagely cut from the womb. I saw mice and rats alike come out from their homes to also see the pamphlets and be filled with joy and a new "freedom" had been granted. Yes, it seemed to me, that so little freedoms remained in our state, that any chance of the people gaining one—no matter how brutish—brought them quick acceptance and delight. As I went back into my house, I saw the authorities march towards me before I could shut the door.

"Are you George Müller?" One asked.

"Yes. What's this about?"

"We have reason to believe your brother had committed a crime in the neighborhood three weeks ago. Our description of the perpetrator was a rat and your brother was seen walking about at night around the same time as the incident occurred." He replied.

My mother then stepped in and overheard the conversation.

"My son was with me that night, it couldn't have been him." She explained.

"We must come in ma'am."

They then plowed through the doorstep and frantically searched the house attempting to find him; meanwhile breaking and throwing our items about. They found him in his room and put him in chains. As they marched down the street, my mother ran after them, pleading his release. The judicial system was heavily corrupt, and the only judges were those appointed by the Society. She knew then, that if tried, he would almost certainly be killed. After yelling at them for some time, she then grabbed one of their arms; truly, a grave mistake. I watched in horror at what came next. Without hesitation, one of the men came up to her and struck a spear through her body. I ran over as fast as I could, but it was too late. I cried with a mix of sorrow and anger. Filled with grief that her life was cut short, and furious at the fact that she, like my brother, was innocent.

NIGHT OF SPEARS
CHAPTER FOUR

IT WAS THE FIRST DAY of fall. I sat at my window reading illegal books and watched through the lighthouses' large window the clouds roll in and turn ever darker by the day. It was comparable to the dusky state of my life and all that which veils the light of the day. That was the only glimpse I had of the outside world. Suddenly I was interrupted by the site of the Castle. There were mice killing other mice, and I knew there was something serious taking place. I quickly ran to the castle and found Owl standing about its cap giving orders to a faction of police on his side. They were common authorities, but they were against their fellow law enforcement. I saw each member of the Ninth Society brought out before the court of the castle with clothes over their faces. For the moment I was confused until the realization of what was happening dawned on me. At once, these "new policemen" came in seemingly in endless droves from some unknown place and slayed as many of the common policemen as possible. They then placed the nine members of the Society in a line and slaughtered each one with spears. They then took the impaled bodies and placed them in front of the iron gate. It was a coup d'etat.

Owl then raised his large wings and lightning flashed outside the lighthouse. His beak grinned and the room became cold. Frantically I ran to Rachel's house. As I was then without a family, I thought it best to see her; perhaps it would be my last chance. I got to her house but she wasn't there and the door was locked. I then saw Owl's mice guards marching down the streets in my direction. Not having enough time to return to my house, I hid behind some garbage cans. The guards' faces were filled with vileness in all ways. Their eyes were glaring and yet their mouths were in the image of sweet pleasure, as though the end-goal of their mission at last came. They had in the hands papers with numerous names. They were death lists. I could hear them converse with one another.

"Is she on the list?" One asked as he approached the porch of a house.

"She's suspected of Anti-Mice-ism." Another answered.

Instantly they broke down the woman's door and raided the house for Anti-Mice paraphernalia. They then took the rat and her family out of the house and hanged them all by a street light cable. I cowered in fear at the site of their deeds. They followed only that which they chose to see, and believed what they had invented. Their leader was Owl, and they were inseparable from him. Owl was for them, Owl was them, and they were Owl. Like a curtain which creates darkness but believes it's on the side facing the light, they were the personification of *Alteration* leading rodent-kind to enlightenment. Yes, they were the gods of their religion; lords of death.

I turned to see the tail of a rat also hiding behind nearby boxes. I quickly and quietly shuffled over to him while the guards weren't looking. The rat turned to face me, and to my surprise it was Rachel!

"What are you doing here?" I whispered.

"I was on my way home from school. They let us out early. Who are these people?" She answered.

"I don't know, but we need to get out of here. Can we get in your house?"

She nodded. We then subtly made our way around a corner and entered the house through the back door.

"We need to hide everything!" I exclaimed.

"Hide what?"

"The books. If they find them we're going to die."

Instantly we searched her whole room, and gathered all the illegal and "immoral" literature we could muster.

"Where are we going to put it?" She asked.

I thought for a moment.

"Do you have a cellar?"

"I do, but do you think we have time?"

"Come on, we have to try."

As fast as possible we took books by the handful down in the dark recesses of the cellar and hid the books behind jars of canned fruit. A knock then came from the door.

"Hurry!" I exclaimed.

The knocking got louder, and we sealed up and locked the door. We then placed a bed on top of it for good measure. I answered the door, and before I could say anything they rushed in and began rummaging the place. We nervously stood and silently watched.

"It's clear." One of the mice said.

I took a sigh of relief, until all of the sudden one of them stopped and looked at a book beneath some papers on a desk. We missed one. My heart sank. He turned the page to discover it was our cherished "Huckleberry Finn". They immediately put cuffs around our feet and led us outside.

A NEW SCHOOL
CHAPTER FIVE

WE MADE OUR WAY DOWN the long black street near nightfall. Along the way, I saw rats taken from their homes and killed with spears and knives. Indeed, they were germs in the bees nest; a dissonance in the melody of the new order. We walked for about seventy feet (a long time in rat-strides) until we approached the school for criminals. It was a re-education camp. I assumed that since our book did not contain anti-mice-ism "propaganda", or any mice characters for that matter, we managed to evade death at their bloody hands.

We approached the barb-wired fence, and I could see the bleak, plain, and small barracks in the distance. Surrounding the compound were large guard-towers manned by mice soldiers equipped with bows and arrows and harpoons. Crude weapons, but they were experts in their skills. There would be no chance of escape.

The re-education camps were nothing new, they existed before Lord Owl came into power. Like a sheep led to the slaughter, I was taken there by my front paws as I began to drag my legs. Up until that point, Rachel had been alongside me. There were numerous rows of camps however, and at the last minute we were separated and she was taken to one farther down the street. It made me sad. I abhorred my situation, but I would have at least found comfort in spending the time in her presence.

The gates opened and I was taken into a room with a mouse in a dark uniform. He read my crimes before me:

"For the acts of committing a crime against the existence of mice and possessing illegal materials containing 'hate-words', you shall be subjected to labor and a new, 'proper education.'"

"Labor" was a gentle euphemism. It would, as I found out in time, become nothing less than grueling enslavement. They pinned me down and shaved my fur; perhaps in order to humiliate me. I was then taken to one of the barracks. There were eight "beds" crammed into the little shack. They were no more than slabs of wood. No blankets or pillows. No toilet, save a bucket. And no lights. The rats in there were quietly laying on their beds resting. They looked to be starving and shaking in the cold air of our ending Autumn. Having nothing else to do, I joined them and tried to get some sleep for the rest of the night.

I was abruptly awoken at what I presumed to be about three in the morning, but I couldn't know for sure. Guards rushed into the room and kicked outside into the cold windy night. We were forced to run around a large dusty track for four hours until morning came. It was as though a cruel joke, that they would make it seem that we were running towards something, perhaps escape. We went nowhere.

After this, we were forced into using machines and manufacturing artillery for the new "police". I would be in charge of making bombs and spearheads. Painstakingly, I would put metal into a hydraulic press. One heavy sheet of metal after another for nine hours straight. When this was finished, we would get a small ration of cheese for the day. It was hardly enough to feed a child, yet it tasted exquisite after such a hard day's work.

The day concluded with "proper education". We were placed into a small wooden room and forced to stand and cramp between one another. Although capable of storing about fifty rodents, one hundred and twenty of us were squeezed together.

"Rats are the tyrants of our lighthouse and holy Alteration. They seek to resurface their suppressive ways of four-score years ago. You all must humble yourselves to the fact that mice are now in charge, and the epoch of rats shall be no longer. Our voices are true and weigh heavier than yours, for we have risen above silence in the face of autocrats. We are the martinets of justice. Be grateful that you are here. Instead of potentially offending mice, by which you are *'harming'* therewith, you have the privilege of being here and becoming enlightened. We will teach you the ways of Mice-ism and respect. Your lord is now Owl. Praise him and give yourselves unto him, for he has led captives free, and liberated the heavy heads of the *'chosen ones'*. We are indebted to him, and owe it to his order that we fulfill his ultimate will of conquering." The teacher pronounced.

It went on like this for four weeks. Wake up, work, learn, and sleep. By the end of it, I had lost nearly a pound and looked emaciated. Thankfully, my fur had partly grown back, and I felt at least a glimpse of warmth as I slept. At the end of each week, a random selection of rats would be granted a meeting with the teachers. Like parole officers, if one could convince them that they had been fully rehabilitated they could have a chance of release. A day before winter, I was given my chance.

I sat before them as they inquired about my place in the lighthouse. I debated in my mind what to say. Would I pretend to agree with their beliefs and have potential to leave, or be honest and continue to suffer? I wanted to be truthful, but I could not stand the toil any longer. Every part of my body ached, and I could feel every bone. I feared that if I stayed, I would surely die of hunger, if not from the cold.

"Who are you?" One of the mice asked.

I relented.

"I am a pest in the house; a smear of dirt on a rug; the bane of rodent-kind." I answered.

They turned to each other and debated amongst themselves.

"Very well." They replied.

A TYRANT'S TUNE

CHAPTER SIX

AS THE GUARDS REMOVED the shackles from my legs, they held me down and branded me with an image of Owl across my back. They then locked a silver ring around my back right paw. It was a symbol of surrender. Those who possessed the ring were those who gave in to mice ideology and Alteration. I was ashamed to wear it, and know that I would wander about the city labeled as a reconditioned mice sympathist.

One of the guards formed a line with the rest of the re-educated ones and I was placed in the very back. At night, we then marched away from the camp towards a large stadium. I could see it from forty feet away. It was now the first day of winter and as snow fell outside the window of the lighthouse, it lit up with the lights of the stadium. When we got there we were amidst death. It was a rally. Around the stadium were lit torches of the hottest flames and banners everywhere with the effigy of a mouse with a spear and shield plastered on them. Every inch of the place was crowded with mice in black uniforms and rats with rings around their ankles. Before them, on an extremely high stone platform, was Owl.

He was different from when I first saw him during the coup. He had grown even bigger and towered over the stadium. His eyes were glowing red and his feathers blackened, upon his head an iron crown. Around him were his head and most loyal guards, and above and behind him was a large statue of a mouse's head with sharp teeth—their new icon. In front of him was a small baby rat chained to the podium.

"Hail Owl! Hail Owl! Praise be unto our lord!" They cried out with tears.

Then Owl stepped up to the microphone and began to speak:

"This winter marks a new time. We are in the era of retribution. Let those around us who wish to stop our order be crushed by the might and weight of our shields. We are like gods over rodent-kind; come to steal the fruits of past labor. We have come to form the correct ways of life, come to be more outspoken than the Ninth Society. The bastardly rats control the economy. They plant their dirty selves in every facet of our lives, and their population exceeds us. They have formed their own separationalist group calling themselves the "Rat Separation Party" (R.S.P.). We shall not stand for their Rat-ist agenda. Rat-ism is now domestic terrorism: kill all whom you suspect of it and inform the police without mercy! Now are the days of the Speech-Police. I will form them and they will walk in the footsteps of our policies. We shall follow the doctrine of Alteration. No more shall rats be allowed to dress in the uniforms of mice, nor marry one another. No more shall women and men be seen as different entities. We are one, and in one Mice-ist revolution we stand! Praise the lighthouse, praise the being of mice!"

"Hail! Hail! Hail! Hail! Hail!" The crowd shouted.

Then Owl bent down and ate the small rat from his shackles. This only made the crowd roar even more. I looked around them all and saw the hundreds of banners waving in the cold windy air. I then saw Rachel in another line. Her fur was shaved and she was shaking. She, too, had a ring about her foot. I dared not attempt to say anything to her, and I could tell she was as frightened as me.

HAIL DEATH
CHAPTER SEVEN

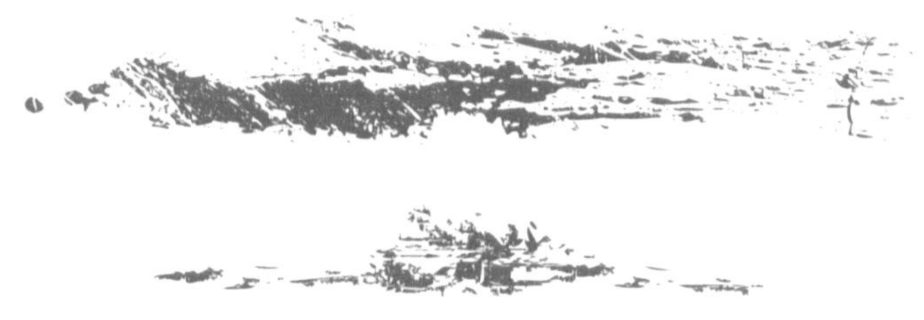

THE RALLY CONCLUDED with a large bonfire before the podium. Dead rat carcasses were thrown into it, and the smell which permeated the air was horribly malodorous. I made my home back home after about a month of being gone. In the streets were mice with flamethrowers raiding houses for any kind of rat book and burning them thus in droves.

On my door, a new pamphlet read:

"Dead rodents,

It shall be thus that any female rat dressed differently from that of males shall be subjected to re-education. The Owl shall provide all with black uniforms, and any who refuse shall be punished swiftly and rightly. All homes shall be herewith be painted black, so that none will be indistinguishable from the next. We are one, and no one shall be individuals separated from our glorious empire. Every rodent will herein be provided jobs by the Owl; payment will be abolished, as Owl shall provide provisions. All weapons are now illegal, save those who are now the police and Speech-Police. Every house must hang the flag of Mice-ism upon the top of their homes and every building. They must all look identical. To conclude, all television will be funded by Owl and directed by the Speech-Police.

Hail the Mice-ist Owl!"

I turned on the television, to see every program filled with forums and mice "intellects" discuss the new economic way of life and how the

Order will redefine the lighthouse for the better. I watched one of these channels.

"Today we are joined by Fred Putney." Said a mouse with glasses and a black uniform sitting on a high chair. "I would like to discuss firstly, the implications of the new laws. Although we all know the moral answer, I would press you on your perspective."

"Well I think the question speaks for itself." Mr. Putney replied. "Men and women are both rodents. They should not have district identities. Before, men could act like women and vice versa; therefore, Owl has, most correctly, eliminated the notion of gender altogether."

"And what about mothers and fathers?" The first mouse asked. "Should they be seen as different?"

"Of course not." He replied. "Verily, I would rephrase the question to *What about 'breeders'?*". The notion of "mothers" and "fathers" is an outdated archaic idea created by rats to create a sense of individual–and divisive, for that matter–identities. Honorable Owl attempts to now reconcile this long-held dogma with Alteration. If anything, a "parent" should be Owl and the Order. They will thoroughly teach correct history, morals, and religion. There is no chance of a rogue *'breeder'* instilling the wrong and dangerous ideals to a child. I would even go so far as to say children ought to be treated more like adults. A Mice-ist mouse child is already superiorly more intellectual than a Rat-ist adult."

"I couldn't have said it better." The other mouse replied.

So appalled and angry, I turned off the screen and refused to watch any show from then on. I then heard a knock at the door. It was two Speech-Police officers holding camera equipment and black outfits.

"Can I help you?" I asked.

"You are required to wear these." One responded.

They then handed them to me and pushed me aside to install the cameras throughout the house.

"If you make any attempt to remove these, you will be sent to a camp."

I simply nodded.

"This is information for your new job. You start in one hour." He said, handing me a stack of papers.

Later that day, I put on my uniform and walked to a building following the address provided. I was told the shift would be twelve hours without breaks and I was placed in a line with four hundred identical rodents. We were in charge of making nails, which would then be distributed evenly throughout the lighthouse, regardless of supply and demand.

WHEN RATS SCREAM
CHAPTER EIGHT

EXHAUSTED FROM THE day of tedious and repetitive labor, I went home again at night to find yet another pamphlet on my door.

"Any mouse previously committed of a crime shall be pardoned hereon." I read.

My eyes turned red with anger as I clenched my fist. They were the personification of all that can go wrong–savages of wickedness and vile orders. Will this madness end? I thought. When shall the brutes reap what they had sown? Like lions who pry and stalk, they impatiently waited for a reason to kill the spirit of my existence. I went to sleep in vexation and downed some alcohol to calm me down.

It was midnight when I was suddenly awoken by the sound of blasts and flaring lights out my window. Quickly, I ran outside to see what was going on. It was rats dressed in white fatigues throwing bombs at the factories, and screaming into the night with glowing torches.

"What's going on?" I asked a nearby mouse.

"It's the Rat Separationalist Party. They've rebelled!"

I swiftly ran inside to turn on the television dn see the news. Every channel was the same broadcast of Owl giving a speech upon the Castle.

"Mice-ists of our Order,

The time has come to win once and for all. The R.S.P. has made it their agenda to instill fear into our peoples. We must crush them with our might! Give no mercy to these beasts! No more is Alteration–I declare Abolition. Kill all rats on sight, for they are the enemy of morality–makers of destruction of order."

I debated what to do next. Would I stay and hide under the rug like a scared worm which fears death in the presence of a bird, or should I remain neutral and allow the whole game to play out. And yet, still, what if I would in fact, join them. I believed what they believed. I wanted the Order killed, and I wanted Owl buried. No, I thought, I would not remain quiet. I would fight, and I would die for the right cause.

IN THE R.S.P.
CHAPTER NINE

As the bombing continued on through the night, I took off my uniform and carefully and slowly moved over towards the R.S.P. I saw a young rat boy around my age fighting and I ran to him.

"I want to help!" I shouted amidst the chaos.

He said nothing but handed me a spear.

The hoards of mice began to increase exponentially shortly thereafter.

"Retreat!" A presumably a rat general yelled.

They all turned back and began running to an unknown destination. I ran with them, not knowing where we could possibly go. Owl and the police had placed surveillance all throughout the state, and I couldn't think of a place free from it. We ran through numerous alleys and corridors in between the dark buildings, until we reached an unsuspicious door just a little off the ground.

"Hurry! Hurry!" One of the rats whispered.

We entered one-by-one into a large cellar fitted into a military bunker. They all sat down being worn out and laid their spears on a table.

"Who are you?" One of the generals asked.

"I want to fight with you." I replied. "I wanted Mice-ism destroyed."

"Great. You're enlisted."

That was easy, I thought to myself. We went over to the table and he handed me a spear.

"Let's get that ring off." He said, as he put a pair of bolt-cutters to it. It made my ankle feel better, and not as though I was tightly cuffed. "We go to war tomorrow. Now rest."

I laid down to get some sleep the rest of the night before the battles began. I could hardly close my eyes thinking about it all, and whether I made the right decision. Was I really prepared to die? And worse, could I really kill someone? The thoughts troubled me more than I had hoped, but I managed to gently drift to sleep after about an hour. The next day, we ate a portion of cheese rations and made our way to the outskirts of the city, where there were only wooden floors. Our brigade, composed of untrained rats like myself, thankfully remained towards the back, so as to let the more experienced soldiers fight first. As we approached we could see what we were up against. Thousands of mice with artillery and weapons ran towards us, and began loading shells. It was, in a sense, and though morbid, beautiful to see the splendor fiery lights ignite in the smoky air above us. We then charged. I dodged countless spears thrown my way, and saw fellow rats not so lucky. I could hardly see through the dust and smoke, it was so thick. My spear was raised but my mind was not in the state to use it.

As I ran I stumbled upon a small mouse child, who appeared to be injured in his left foot. Would this be it? I thought. Should I fulfill my duty and end him? I looked around me and made the most rational decision I do think I had ever made in my life. I threw my spear down and picked up the child. I ran towards our side until I saw other rats coming in and out of a hole in one of the floorboards.

"What are you doing?" Asked one of them.

"He's hurt and just a child." I said.

"Alight, come on." He replied.

I took him in and tended to his wounds, which I found to be a broken leg. He was shivering and crying.

"Why did you save me?" He asked.

I thought about it for a minute. Perhaps I didn't even know why I did, it just seemed like the right thing to do.

"You don't know what you're doing." I said. "Don't be like them. A rodent should help his fellow rodent, and you don't deserve to die."

After caring for him, I wrote a letter to the general asking him to spare the mouse's life and allow him to stay with us; that he did no wrong and didn't deserve to be treated as a Mice-ist. I then rested the rest of the night alongside him.

"Wake up, boy." A rat said, standing over me. "The general would like to see you."

I woke up and went with the man, until we were in the presence of a large rat in fatigues.

"Were you the one who wrote this?" The general asked, holding up the letter.

"I did, sir."

"You're an exquisite writer, I must say. You believe we should spare his life?"

"I do." I responded.

"And you think he's done no wrong? That he's not a threat?" He asked.

"That's right sir, I don't believe he's a danger. He's just a boy."

"Very well." He replied after a moment of deep thought.

He came over to me and shook my paw.

"You're a hero, kid. You read, do you?"

"Quite a lot." I replied. "I read illegal books."

"Then you know the true origin of Mice-ism and Rat-ism?" He asked.

"I know that they were different times; that each had their places in society until Mice-ism sought vengeance, and corrupted history with the religion of Alteration."

"Then we can use you." He responded. "You're not going to fight, you're going to write."

REWRITING TRUTH
CHAPTER TEN

"What would you like me to write?" I asked the general.

"I want you to make a memoir of this lighthouse. Detail everything, and rewrite our false-history of Alteration. Explain the uncorrupted truth of Mice-ism. Will you do it?"

"I will." I said.

"Good. Matthew, hand the boy some paper." He said to an officer.

I spent the rest of the night writing as much as I could. I was no longer sympathetic. I spoke the truth. I wrote about the dangers of Alteration and how it threatens liberty. I wrote about the evil of Owl and the Speech-Police. In two months I managed to write a good sized novel.

"I've done it." I said as I gave the papers to the general. "It's finished."

He read over it for about an hour, all the while having a smile on his face.

"It's perfect!" He exclaimed. "I want everyone in the R.S.P. to have a copy. I wanted them to know what they're fighting for. You're now to be the face of our party. Like Owl, you will be our spokesperson."

I began to fulfill my duties as the adjutant of my general. Every night we would hold a meeting amongst members of the party and I would give speeches and orations of my book to great applause. It made them happy knowing that there was someone there to give them a real voice. Indeed, it was as though I was their own Owl. A great irony I thought. During such meetings, we would get further intel on the affairs of rodents living in the new Order.

"Things have since gotten worse in these last weeks." An officer stood and exclaimed. "They have begun a frenzy hunting down your books and burning them, sir. They have taken blood from the battlefields of rats and smeared it across the doors of their loved ones."

"We ought to collect their blood!" Another stood and said.

"No, we cannot." I replied. "We must not sink ourselves to their level."

"I fear we must succumb to their tactics and embrace their savage ways if we are to win the war." Another said.

"If we've learned anything from true history, it is that there's always another way and we can accomplish it through peaceful means." I said.

"Are you really so confident as to think they'll lay down and die, nevermind surrender?"

"What do you propose then, George?" He asked.

"I say we perform another coup." I replied.

"But how can such a thing be done? There's too many guards, they see it coming from a mile away."

"We need a distraction." I said. "If we have someone get the attention of Owl and the mice during one of their rallies, we can storm the castle."

"But what will be the distraction?"

I thought about it for a minute.

"We need someone in charge. If they can approach Owl and offer surrender for all to see, they might buy it."

"Who will do it? Who will risk such a thing?" He asked.

The room went silent and no one stepped up. Then, for a reason unknown to me; perhaps of sudden boldness or inherent leadership, I lifted my chest.

"I'll do it." I exclaimed.

THE CONQUEROR
CHAPTER ELEVEN

WITHOUT WASTING TIME, we prepared every brigade that night. The plan was for a select squadron to ambush the backside of the Castle while I distracted Owl. Then, while the mice cheered and Owl smiled, the whole party would attack the ralliers. At three in the morning we made our way.

As we approached the grand Castle we dug holes underground to bypass the fence. The rats then hid under the floorboards until they heard the crowd cheer at my sight. I then left them and made my way swiftly up the stairs. It all came to me in the moment what I was really doing and what led me there. I went from being a meek schoolboy to the face of a confederate army in mere months. Would this be it? I thought. Would this be the night when I finally met my end? No, I told myself. This can't be it. What if I succeeded? What if the rats actually won and Alteration was destroyed?

I got to the top level of the tower and saw the darkest sights in the coldest air of January. Like months prior, they all hailed Owl and sang praise. Around the god were dead rat bodies for which the generals took turns sticking spears into them. They would then dip their flags in their blood. I took a deep breath and prepared myself for what I was about to do. I took out my white flag and some rope. Instantly I threw it over the balcony and descended with the flag in my mouth. I jumped onto the stage and saw everyone gasp with shock that I dared come. Owl, wearing his evil face, then looked down on me with his fiery red eyes. I fiercely began waving the flag.

"We surrender! We surrender!" I shouted. "Praise Owl!"

The crowd went silent for a brief moment, perhaps waiting for what their leader would think. Then Owl smiled and the crowd erupted in applause and victorious joy. They believed they won. As soon as the cheers could be heard, the squadron stormed the Castle from beneath the floorboards and signaled the R.S.P. army to approach.

The mice looked in horror at their foolish unpreparedness. Nearly twenty percent were slaughtered in the first fifteen minutes before they could raise up their weapons. I saw then, Owl rise up and spread his wings. He gave a large screech and began killing my rats with his long talons. Eventually, at some point, he fixed his eyes on me. I tried to run but he was too fast. I saw his large gaping beak bend down to swallow me up. Then it happened.

In some inexplicable force of God, there came upon the lighthouse a loud thud. The voice of every rodent; every mouse, rat, and Owl, became silent. At once, for the first time in our history, the seven-foot door to the building opened.

"A human! Run!" Everyone shouted.

But the man entered too quickly and he saw us all amidst the battle. He was a scruffy man, perhaps in his late thirties, holding an oil lamp and foodstuffs. His disposition was beyond confused and bewildered. His eyes instantly widened and he was taken aback in shock.

Then Owl saw him and the might of his stature. Without a thought, Owl spread his great wings and flew to attack the face of the man; he who could overshadow his power. He screeched dreadfully and the man shouted.

"Leave! Leave!" Owl cried, as he stuck his claws into the man's face.

The man grabbed Owl by his feet, and brought him over to the window. At once he threw him into the glass and outside. I saw then,

Owl be struck by lightning in the raging storm abound. He fell from grace, down below into the abyss of the outside world.

We all stared at the man, fearful and yet curious. Indeed, at that moment we stopped frightening. Their leader was dead, and our enemy was falling. Perhaps we were equals then. Neither of us had morale to fight, and the man was the new threat in any case. He curiously walked over to our city and bent down to see us.

"Who are you?" He asked himself.

"Who are *you*?" A particularly bold mouse responded.

"You can speak!" He exclaimed. "What is going on here? How did you get here? How can you speak?"

"We are the chosen ones of the lighthouse. We do not know our history." Another mouse said. "Will you be our god?"

"Your god?" The man replied. "I'm no god."

"But you are so big and intelligent. Surely you can guide us."

"That owl, just now. Was that your god?"

"He was, sir. He was our messiah." The mouse said.

"Look what he did to my face. You would follow such a thing? Look at yourselves; you're killing each other–for what?"

"For Mice-ism. The rats are evil, they once controlled everything. Mice are far more superior."

"Well you're both tiny pests to me. I don't see anything more special in a rat than a mouse." He responded.

We all put our heads down, perhaps out of shame or feeling so small. I thought about Rachel and my family at that moment. I wonder what she was thinking seeing the man. If she remained frightened or looked at him with optimism. At least I knew that I could again see her knowing this war was finally over. Then I dreamt about my mother and my brother. If only they were alive to see this. When the age of oppression ended only a few seasons later.

"I'll tell you what." Said the man. "I'm going to be living here for the next year. I could teach you history, and show you the right way to live. I could show you how to live in harmony."

I saw the people then look at one another and smile. I knew from then on we would live in peace. I could go home, see Rachel, and for the first time, sleep soundlessly without fear.

The
Ants

The nameless man sat upon his bed, despondent and ashamed while he buried his face in his hands. Beside him lay the gun he'd utilized not more than a minute prior. After his ducts had exhausted all the tears, he forced himself to remove the palms and acknowledge the scene.

In front of him was the stalker, the fiend. He had broken into Nameless' house with a knife wielded tightly in his hands, ready to lunge viciously at Nameless. The latter, living man, knew quite well the reason.

Nameless knew he himself had once worked for the CIA and, upon getting unexpectedly fired, stole a stack of top-secret military documents. He was not being followed for no reason. Nameless plucked the courage to examine the body closer–making sure his speculations were true. In the man's pocket, he found a police badge; it was certain. The police department, as Nameless knew, were colluding with the CIA and out to get him, lest he release the information to the public.

He felt disgusted with himself; both that he put himself in the dangerous situation and moreso that he had killed a human. He quickly rushed to the bathroom to wash his hands. They were clean, but iniquitous filth stuck to the fingers.

As he scrubbed viciously and watched ants wander about the sink, he caught a brief glimpse of the man's shadow behind him through the mirror. Of course, it wasn't real, he thought. He assumed it to be a minor hallucination from an extraordinarily traumatic and stressful event. He dismissed his mind and returned to the body for some semblance of contemplation as to resolve the unresolvable incident.

Nowhere to his surprise, the body was already infested with ants who took morsels of his bloody flesh. Nameless lived alone in an old house built without a foundation; it was, therefore, exceedingly common for ants and spiders to creep in every corner of the meek homestead.

It was about then that he felt the ants crawling up his clothes quickly. Already panicked, he threw off his jeans and long-sleeve shirt out of agitation, went to the backyard, and lit them on fire. Still perturbed, and with a mix of sorrow, apprehension, and slight confusion, he chose to return inside wearing only his black boxers.

Thinking of no escape by himself, Nameless decided to call up Hunter. He had been best friends with Nameless since childhood and just so happened to be a co-worker at the CIA, as Nameless remembers. If any would know what to do, it'd be him; at least, provided he was still a friend.

In an instant, Hunter arrived and attempted to mollify the killer.

"Calm down." Said Hunter. "Show me where it happened."

They both walked into the room.

"These damned ants everywhere." Said Nameless. "The body and floor are ripe with them."

To Nameless' complete shock, Hunter looked at him in silence, demanding slowly the words, "Where is he? There's no one here."

Nameless couldn't utterly believe his ears. He knew something more was going on—something deeper, something sinister.

"Hunter," said Nameless, "you can't be serious. I trust you more than anyone and you know I have my head most comfortably on my shoulders. What are you trying to pull?"

"Why don't you let me see these supposed documents." Replied Hunter.

At this point, Nameless was hesitant. He already came to suffer shock at his friend's foolery and deception. Still, he handed him only the cover page, ensuring not even he knew the full content.

"Are you joking, Nameless? This is just a bunch of scribbles and word-salad. Why don't you give me the rest so I can really gauge what you mean."

Nameless was naturally already furious by then and wasn't prepared to give Hunter one more word. He seemed almost to be in on it too and wanted the papers out of the home. Surely, the CIA would employ his best friend to reobtain the classifieds; it made sense. He gave Hunter a vexed, strange look.

In a calm manner, as though receiving a revelation, Nameless said, "So now even you are a part of it; of all the years we spent working together."

"Don't be silly, Nameless. You've never worked at the CIA with me. You got laid off from the Better Mart down the street a month ago."

Nameless was speechless. He simply couldn't fathom what sort of trick Hunter was playing on him. The CIA was more than known for mind control and top-notch persuasion, but Nameless wouldn't fall for it. He'd been trained himself on the matter and wasn't prepared to give into the tactics.

"You bastard." Is all Nameless could mutter.

"Look," said Hunter, "Why don't you go into the other room. I'll take care of these ants in here and clean up your room while you calm down."

Nameless did so, making sure to keep the documents tightly with him in his grasp. He could only hear miscellaneous noises coming from the other side of the door. He tried to settle his mind, but, when you know you're innocent and one's own government is out to get you, fear and unease sets in and strangles.

"There we are." Said Hunter. "Come out and sit."

As Nameless slowly opened the door, he found the body and ants gone but the pool of blood remaining, soaked into the carpet. Hunter held the knife in his hand and swished it up and down as he made it all very clear to Nameless.

"Now look. You know I care about you," said Hunter with a stern voice, "and I'm telling you to get yourself together and do what's in your best interest. Don't go mentioning anything about this 'murder' or acquiring of secret knowledge. You've already lost most of your family. Say anything and they'll throw you in an institution and subject your head to electroshock therapy. Do you want that? Besides, no one will believe you; but you still need to watch your steps. Those documents aren't real and you're best to hand them over to me. It'll relieve your psychotic paranoia and make you less crazy."

Mayhaps they were guiltless comments, but Nameless took them as mince threats and could only look towards Hunter's eyes with arrogance and fury–no longer disbelief. There was no way he was prepared to hand over those documents to a CIA agent, he thought.

Hunter set the knife down and turned to leave when he suddenly stopped.

"Oh! I almost forgot." He said. "Seeing as I was coming over and wasn't worried anything bad actually occurred, I nabbed your old trophy from when we were kids and thought to return it to you."

The trophy was that of a medium-sized crow with a plague beneath it. It simply read, "To The First Place Winner".

Nameless knew with complete certainty that he never owned the trophy; he'd never won first place in anything. Hunter set it down so as the eyes of the crow were pointed directly at him.

"Get well, Nameless. Enough with these documents." He said as he exited the home.

Nameless just took a seat and stared at the crow. Hunter removed the body–that was a fact, Nameless thought.

"The bird's eyes." He thought while looking onward at the crow. "I know there's a camera in them. We've done this trick many times on unsuspecting citizens. I won't let them get me, no matter what."

The
Shabby Sod

Y ou shabby sod! What are you doing and why have I let you into my hovel? I ask myself. No, I should not have done that. I sit before you on the other chair in my so-called 'fancy' living space–as I am fond of putting it. You sick, confusing derelict. You stare at me without closing of eyes; without moving of lips nor hands. What are you? Crazy? Medically ill? Exhausted from living on the streets? In any case, I'm clueless and without words as to why you emulate a robot and inquired about staying the night. I was kind, do you not see? Letting you in for a cup of hot tea with two sugars and company? Indeed, the least you can do is humor and acknowledge me, in my own gracious home! Speak, move you rote visage of a human!

I'm now beginning to get paranoid. What is wrong? I've never felt this way before. Is he–this shabby sod, of whom I know not his very name–reading my mind or controlling me of the sorts? He did not act this way when I met him whilst walking home from work. I sympathized with you, having been in gross debt in my early days. You were so sweet; so kind, so lighthearted and tearful, but everso optimistic in a contracting way. Speak! I'm talking to you! Do you not want your tea? I'm cooking you some toast and it shall get warm if you cannot even open your filthy, raggedy-haired mouth (or a maw?).

I'm gritting my teeth at this point. My hands and feet are sweating while chills flow swiftly through my standing hairs. You don't even notice, do you? You seem unable to sense fear–or any feelings for that matter. You only stare attentively and (frankly) menacingly into my eyes. Not one blink in two full minutes. It's as though you've suddenly died, but your soul has failed to leave your flesh. Am I going crazy? Absolutely not.

The doctor informed me yesterday that I should be cautious: both of the people I interact with and those who pose odd mannerisms or thinking. Why he said that, I cannot say, but strange things are happening, and it would appear that my doctor is some hidden psychic. Damn! You sod! You've made me nervous to drink my tea, despite my grave thirst. Perhaps you poisoned it when I wasn't looking. Based upon my newfound observance of your alien demeanor and changed personality, you could be a serial killer for all I know. True, the homeless do not oft seek out home-owners as prey; it's quite the opposite usually. Nevertheless, I cannot bear this torturing unease. I no longer trust him and want him out of my sight. Period.

That's it, leave! I'm commanding his departure in the strictest sense and without empathy. You are creepy and not welcome here. I don't want you hanging around!

Still, the man does not even flinch. Ought I call the cops? I do wonder, however, and the thought does indeed cross my mind that there may be curious things happening to the police, just as much. Why do I think this, you ask? Well, I should spill the beans, seeing as we're on the subject and I nearly fear for my life. I feel that I can trust you just as much as my own mind.

You see, as I was walking home from my doctor (whose specific specialty I shall not disclose), I caught a glance of the police walking down Meridian Street. I generally take the backroads, you understand, or the alleys due to my anxiety. But, I was intrigued, for whatever reason, so I strolled over to them. To my shock (maybe awe), they were marching with peculiar weapons I've never beheld. Despite being in common police uniforms, naturally, they moved like soldiers and held their guns in the most intimidating of ways. Taken aback and alarmed, I quickly escaped back into the shadows of the alley.

This all makes me consider–and yes, I admit to you that this is very, *very* far-fetched–that the people around me are actually robots in disguise. Ludicrous! Or, what if the world has been plagued/invaded by aliens? This isn't in my head and I'm more aware of my surroundings than ever.

This is what I'll do, okay? My doctor, who specializes in these matters, explained that I need to avoid these people. I will walk gently to the bathroom, lock the door, and wait for him to leave. Now I know this sounds moronic. A homeless man willingly leaving a home he has been invited into? Ha! How idiotic to think such a thing, but I trust the doctor who says he knows a thing about robots and aliens.

Okay, I'm walking. The man's eyes are following mine, but I'm trying to ignore him. I've made it to the bathroom. Take deep breaths, lock the door, and act like everything's natural, I tell myself. I hear footsteps...

Stay relaxed, close your eyes, banish the silly notions of alien/robot domination. That's all I can do, I'm telling myself.

Finally, to my relief, I hear the footsteps cease and the front door open. The doctor really does know what he's talking about. Maybe he's a rogue assisting us poor humans. I'll never know; do you?

The
Undisclosed
Messenger

The man, whom we shall refer to as only, "WRITER"–seeing as his name has little importance in his new, most melancholic life that, in his mind, is worthless–sat both lonesome and red-eyed at his computer. Indeed, he hoped to type one last short story before the incident would occur. Would it be WRITER's magnum opus? He could only hope; yet, none of it would matter after his upcoming meeting with MURDERER.

The poor, tired man was soon to fall asleep at his laptop, just as he was about to type, "Fin.", when, unexpectedly and quite peculiarly, he heard the ring/ping alarming him that he had a new email.

Now, seeing as WRITER possessed the name of his profession, it was not at all unusual to receive query replies, announcements from publishing houses, editorial letters, and all of the sort. And yet, the hand on the wall's clock read midnight. What a strange time to receive a message, he knew.

WRITER's heart sank as he opened his email only to find a single file, reading, "Hello, WRITER". Intrigued, he opened it, finding that the address on it was a series of numbers. Assuming the sender to be a scammer, he half-chuckled but, out of boredom, thought he'd humor him.

"Who is this?" WRITER asks.

The mysterious messenger informs me that, somehow, he knows me: your humble, earnest narrator, WRITER. In no detailed terms, he wants to "help" me. With what? Yes, I will never listen to what my readers say, no one can help with the recent events that have taken place as of late. She'll never come back, what has been cannot be undone, and there's only one option left.

Again, I strictly demand, "Who is this?"

He tells me that he/she wishes to go by, "UNDISCLOSED"–a pseudonym, of course. No matter.

WRITER began to worry and feel uneasy when UNDISCLOSED mentioned that he knew his plans and motives.

Ha! Whoever this clown is doesn't know my motives; surely, he doesn't understand the backstory behind it, if he did. Otherwise, he'd sympathize with me and know that what I'm about to do is justice, perhaps not so-called, "divine justice". This is man's hardy, icy justice: most fitting for the coldness of MURDERER.

A new email popped up–

"Of all the stories you have written thus far in your long life, WRITER, have you never incorporated the theme of: *revenge is never the answer*? That there are always other ways?"

Suddenly, and for no apparent reason, WRITER had the urge to glance over at his bed. Why?

I can't put my finger on the reason, but I went over and pulled out the pistol stashed away beneath my mattress. Ping! I hear a new message.

"Would your WIFE approve of that?" UNDISCLOSED asks.

WRITER, at this point, was infuriated.

How the hell does this clown know about WIFE? The incident wasn't on the news and not many caught wind of it. What's he trying to pull? Her murder was not long ago.

A dark thought began to brew in WRITER's mind. What if UNDISCLOSED was MURDERER? WRITER knew his identity well–having been his family friend for so many years. The police could never pin WIFE's death on him, but WRITER knew the truth.

Bastard! I can't help but think he's MURDERER. "Well then," I write, "I'm soon on my way. Just got to finish the damned story, if I get the time. How you know what's coming eludes me, but rest assured, that gun is waiting for you."

It was at this moment when WRITER's angry grip loosened from his coffee cup that was on the verge of breaking.

"Do you remember our first date?" Asked UNDISCLOSED.

I don't know what to think. Dear audience, my dear readers, being in the trade that I am, I'm a fairly down-to-Earth man and know the various lessons of life: such is what molds a proper writer to tell good tales. But,

I do admit, that I'm more confused than ever, and am utterly bewildered at this whole scenario.

"You were once so caring when with WIFE." Writes UNDISCLOSED. "At that time–during your first date–you wouldn't hurt a fly, for you were truly the kindest of men."

"How do you know about this?" I ask.

"I got with you from that day forth because of that tender fact." Said UNDISCLOSED.

WRITER paused to catch his breath. If this were MURDERER, why would he say this? How would he know any of these details? MURDERER was too young and wasn't alive at that time. Could this be, dare I even consider it, WIFE?...

"I will always love you, WRITER", says "UNDISCLOSED". "I will forever cherish the gentle man I know. I'm in a good, most beautiful place and, if you deal with MURDERER, if you follow the path of misty revenge, we'll be separated for eternity."

Could this all be real? Could this be WIFE? I must ask you, my audience, because this stretches the mind, too much for one individual alone to endure. Is WIFE really communicating with me from beyond the beyond? If so, I trust her motives more than my own. A tear can't help but slowly fall down my cheek. "I love you, WIFE", I write.

One final email popped up following this: "Forever and always, even after death".

Directly after WRITER finished reading it, all the emails got miraculously deleted, and the email address could no longer be found.

I'm sitting silently right now, pondering and awestruck. She was absolutely right. Seeking the death of MURDERER may seem like the right thing to do, but will I be a murder if that occurs? Will I be damned for eternity because of my hatred? No, UNDISCLOSED, WIFE or not, is right. I'll throw the pistol in the river outside my cabin.

When WRITER returned to his bedroom, he was caught off guard to see a picture of WIFE and himself during their wedding night lying upon his bed. As tears continuously fell down hot, red cheeks, he lay down for the night whilst grasping the photo, thanking existence that she saved his soul.

He
Who Lets
The Cows Escape

Mr. Hinnep looked doubtful at the kid leaning against the stable, who proclaimed to have finished his work early.

"And ya got the pens washed too, have ya?" He asked.

"Yes, Mr. Hinnep." The boy said.

"And the sheep shaved? How 'bout the corner fence all up 'n ready?"

"Yes sir, it's all taken care of." Ralph, the boy, said smiling, knowing the farmer would be satisfied with his work.

"Alright kid, that's a good job then. And you're here the rest of the night while the boys and I go out, correct?"

Ralph nodded, not particularly pleased with that aspect of his work, but knew it would be simple and quiet work, which he enjoyed. He was tired from the long, hot day of working in the stables, and (if he had to work) somewhat looked forward to the cool, breezy night ahead of him. The farmer was to be away, and his job would be to tend the livestock and supervise them until the morning. A simple enough job—provided the lay person not know Mr. Hinnep well at all. He was a strict, elderly man, who preoccupied himself with tedious tasks and an unwavering work ethic which he passed down onto his employees–Ralph especially. No one ever dared to question him, nor did they ever complain. After all, they were getting paid to do their jobs, and most assumed it was all he had to ruminate over with no wife or kids.

When the man left, Ralph did as he was told: tending the livestock, and monitoring for stray coyotes who desired to ambush them. The majority—350 to be exact—of the lot were cows owned by the city. At one point in time, the city was low on money at the time, and the decision to transfer all cows into one section of land and sell the remaining farmlands seemed appropriate. This of course, provided the city's boys excellent opportunities for farmhand jobs.

He fixed himself a plate of food left out for him by Hinnep, and sat on the porch to watch the sunset descend over the nearby hills, recalling how the farmer once kept him for three consecutive days, recleaning and re-bleaching a horse stall that did not fit his strict standards. He'd done hard work for the man, but it had made him a hard kid in return, and for that he was grateful. He watched and contemplated for a few hours, until eventually accidently falling asleep. When he awoke, dawn had not quite yet risen. Neglecting his duties, he quickly transferred the cows, fed them, and went off to his house to get ready for school. To his mistake, however, and unbeknownst to him, was the small yet important failure of locking the gate behind him.

When the farmer returned, he noticed immediately that the cows were missing. Upon looking for Ralph, and to no avail, he then went out in search of them himself. Of the few he found, all were dead. Most likely caused by snakes or wolves, but remains a mystery even to this day. The rest, he figured, had succumbed to the same fate or were horribly lost. Shortly afterwards, and with great reluctance explaining the situation to the various owners of the cows, the man quickly fell into eventual bankruptcy. Outraged by this, Mr. Hinnep ran to his city hall, barged the doors open, and demanded to speak with the mayor. Now it was, incidentally, that precise moment when the mayor was in a meeting with another rancher. This one however, was a very wealthy farmer from Nevada, who was on the brink of signing a crucial deal with the city. A deal, which would also include donating a great deal of cattle, thereby producing a generous amount of income for the town. The rancher wished to hold his cattle there during the winter months. Yet, when overhearing that the city's only farmer had lost all of its cows, the rancher suddenly rejected the offer and left annoyed.

At that point, both Hinnep and the mayor were, needless to say, beyond panicking: the farmer, being upset at his bankruptcy, and the mayor as having already completed numerous extravagant city projects with money that was to be repaid on the failed deal. Knowing the city essentially no longer had any money via the selling of the cows and their meat, and having nowhere else to turn to, the two drove to Ralph's house, where they promptly questioned him about the cattle. He was confused, as he thought surely, he must've locked the gate. This did not settle well with the farmer, however, who lashed out at the boy, cursing at him, and even trying to hit him. Seeing this, the mayor began berating the kid, as well. His parents, seeing this, quickly shut the door on them. They themselves, although angry, did not scorn the boy nearly as much and sent him off to school as usual.

When he got to school, he had forgotten about the morning's matter. He sat at a table with his friend Isabelle, getting lunch, and discussing the strangeness of meeting the mayor so informally and unexpectedly. The lunch itself was even odd, as well. The food being only half the portion sizes as normally served.

"Mr. Hinnep and the mayor came to my house this morning." Ralph told her, knowing it'd spark her interest.

"Oh yeah? Why was that?"

"I'm not sure exactly. They asked if I had forgotten to shut a gate behind me when I was working there last night. I don't know what could be so important to have the mayor with them, though. At any rate, I was sure I did."

"That is weird," she replied, "maybe some cows escaped, and they were the mayor's?"

"Perhaps, I suppose you're probably right. I feel bad, if that is what it was."

"You shouldn't feel bad, it was just an accident." She commented, trying to make him feel better.

"I suppose." Ralphed picked at his food, "Hey! Did you still want to go to the docks tomorrow?"

By now the bell had rung and the kids were instructed to return to their classrooms. This too, unusual, as it would generally ring later.

"That sounds like fun, let's do it." She said, as her last words before walking away.

In the classroom, a war began to break out. The teacher was absent, and without one to keep order, the students were free to do as they pleased. One suggested they simply leave; another speculated as to what could've happened to her; and others who told the class to behave as though they were the teachers themselves. Even Ralph—being the kid he was—chose shenanigans, until one student looking out the window decried what would be in hindsight a fearful message to the class.

"Look! The teachers, they're walking out!"

When Ralphed looked, the words were indeed true. The majority of the staff were angrily marching out of the school—appearing as if they were striking, due to their no longer getting paid. Soon, a principal's announcement echoed through the intercom. He told the students to remain calm, and wait patiently for their teachers. Doing as they were told, they waited until the end of the school day, where they likewise left. All were either forced to walk or drive personally, as the buses mysteriously failed to show. Ralph walked along the street towards his home, where he was confronted with the sight of frantic people crowding the city hall. Some were calm; but most had the looks of savages on their faces. Those with government-paid jobs scorned the mayor for the city's inability to pay them. Consequently, store and local business owners ridiculed them for no longer purchasing their products. Only a percentage of the city's people gathered, but all could be seen peering out of their windows. Many joining without hesitation.

This sight scared the boy (knowing he was the cause), and he swiftly rushed the rest of the way. Yet his house was to be no less spiteful. When he entered, he saw his parents in the kitchen—viciously screaming at one another over the loss of their jobs. When Ralph's mother noticed him, her scowl instantly turned in his direction. She began insulting him, and describing how the chaos was his fault for not shutting the gate. This brought him to tears, and he indeed felt entirely helpless about the situation. Around her, he could then see his father angrily break a wooden broom in half in the distance. Ralph quickly ran out the door, fearful of what his father would do next.

It was now in the evening, and the street was wrought with shadows and utter chaos. All of the city's people had now come from their houses and rioted, to say the least. The city hall was in flames, and cars were being smashed, beaten, and flipped over, due to the people having no more money or the ability to buy and sell. Having nowhere to turn to, Ralph ran to Isabelle's house in hopes of not being caught. He knew she would not be mad, but the same could not be said with the rioters. On his way, Mr. Hinnep—who now looked to be a terribly torn, animalistic, and desperate man—spotted him, and screamed to the hungry crowd that Ralph was the boy who let the cows escape. Like packs of wolves and snakes, they began to chase after him.

Even so, he managed to make it to her home, and frantically rushed through the door. When he entered, he saw Isabelle with her grandfather. They hugged each other, and she went on to explain that her parents, too, had joined the frenzy; but her grandfather had not, and felt sympathy for Ralph's mistake. For the fact she had not turned against him, he was happy, but rushed her that they must leave. At the same moment, the mob broke into the house and, like the beasts of the field they were, tore the boy from them, including any valuables on his person. As they stormed out with him, she stood at the doorway crying, while her grandfather simply sat and stoked a fire, apparently without fear of the savages. They threw the boy onto a large platform in the dark street and wrapped a noose around his neck.

"Grandpa! Please do something! You can stand up for him against the crowd and say otherwise!" She yelled.

"Listen Isabelle," he explained calmly, "if I did, they would certainly kill me. Changing nothing."

"That's why nothing changes!" She screamed. "Everyone, like you, has that same mindset. You're afraid to confront them."

"Would you go do it then?" He asked.

She looked down at the ground in tears and silence, softly shutting the door to the scene of Ralph being hanged outside.

The
Margaret
Lincoln Tragedy

The tragedy of Margaret Lincoln is a difficult one to understand. Not least of all, by its unique and curious nature—but also that it occurred to none other than the most innocent and random of young ladies, in the most innocent and random of places. And yet, despite the strangeness of it, it can be rest assured that when seen through the correct eyes, the events of her life were in fact, entirely, and perhaps metaphorically, true.

The homestead of this Ms. Lincoln was atop the grassy and wheat-covered hill of Winter County on the south end of the pacific Harrington Island. An old, small wooden house built by her late grandfather, it was a humble, most unattractive home on the island . There, she lived the whole of her eighteen-year life with her sister and mother. The sister, Mary, was their personal gardener. Introverted and dallying, she felt in all ways complete with her daily routine of planting the petunias, trimming the bushes, and watering the strawberries. Her mother on the other hand, was a prominent artist, whose work had never quite taken off. Though once a week on the same day and same hour she would frequent town to sell her work, it was a rarity to sell even a third of them. Ambitious in her youth, the spark of creation which once enlightened her being with self-assurance and purpose, had all but dimmed to a light ember. Indeed, the dream of Warhol-esque fame was instead replaced by the necessity of providing for the family, a small income an artist oft comes to expect. It was a small income, but an income nonetheless, and for that they were appreciative. Though under the guidance of the two, Margaret (who was a fair deal younger) would come not to desire a career of wealth nor that of a businesswoman as they hoped. It was she whom they felt could raise the state of their wealth and namesake—to succeed in the dreams which long ago failed them. Margaret, however, wanted none of it. She felt no desire to be renowned, and even less so to be rich. Yet that is not to say she lacked ambition. Margaret was a dreamer—having perhaps dreamt more than any of her peers, and the aspirations she desired could never be satisfied with the mere value of financial gain, a large house, or even a steady job. Such reflected her personality, and naturally, said lofty dreams would often be met with scoffs by her peers. The consensus was generally the same: too much hoping and contemplating was time unduly wasted; that she dreamt too much and lost sight of the present. For how can one find their place in the world, when they never escape their head?

"You should go to King Point college, Margaret. Mr. Peterson of the Buy-'n-Go mentioned it to me earlier. It's not expensive and within walking distance. Mary and I have put aside some money for classes. It's time for you to find a job and settle down, don't you think? Make a living, Margaret—a name for yourself, and finally grow up. You cannot be a kid of this house forever. Dusk 'til dawn your sister and I work. We've grown up." Her mother said, while the three of them ate around the dinner table.

She sat quietly, staring at her mashed carrots recently harvested from the garden, and thought over her mother's words. They weren't the words she wanted to hear, nor ones she agreed with, but they had to be considered. The drab life of being barred to one's small home was a simple one, but it was without ambition, and certainly not one to fill the void of her dreams. After a bit of thought, her face lit with an optimistic smile and by any means necessary, she vowed to succeed in her aspirations and prove the fulfillment of them to her mother and sister.

"Alright!", she declared, "I'll make something of myself and will become neither a gardener nor an artist. I'll become a symbol of hope for our quaint island. I'll inspire them to do more than farming and fishing, and change the world for the better, if I can."

She then left the room without a second word. Her family, doubtful, yet surprised by her quick change in initiative, were still thankful at the thought of her getting a job and at last contributing financially.

Incidentally, the change of Margaret's mind came from the very heart of who she wanted to be—a conduit for *opportunity*. From birth she wanted to see the world. To go out, help people, and have fun doing so. Little did she concern herself with ego, money, and power; all of which she lacked. Instead, her focus was on the potential to experience all that lay outside of her creaky bedroom and well-tended gardens. Of these many world-experiences, one in particular did feel very keen on. Unequivocally, free of regret, it was to become a teacher. Being the mild, withdrawn girl she was, and there of course rarely being any on the farm, you understand, she was exceptionally disposed to not seeing children. She admired them for their innocence, and knew no better harbingers of opportunity. Teaching them valuable ideas could surely change the world, and none had more potential. Without any hesitation then, she threw on her jacket, settled onto her bike, and rode into town before dusk. Excited for a life beyond the quiet, old walls of her home, she eagerly rushed into the office of the town's only primary school and filled out an application to become a teacher's assistant.

As she rode home in the warm sunlight following this, her future of becoming a teacher for countless children was sure to come to fruition. She imagined the best teacher from her past—Mr. Brown—and speculated how to best emulate him while incorporating her own visions. And what more did Margaret possess, than a head filled with unbounded visions.

"Perhaps I'll play music," she thought, "and we'll sing songs! If the kids have had a good, productive day, I may even bring them candy. We can write stories and think up our futures."

So it was, that on the night before the first day of autumn, Ms. Lincoln went to bed in a happy state, and would dream dreams not unlike those which she'd always had. She imagined her future self: recommending books for young minds, and helping them to read. They were the dreams only the dreamers of dreams could stir up, and they glowed with a golden hue. When morning came, she rushed down to her phone where a message indicating that she had, in fact, gotten the job was left. Utterly delighted, she again put on her best clothes, and rode to the school as swiftly as the day prior.

As she entered, she was greeted with the scent of carved pumpkins, and a plethora of children welcoming her into their classroom.

"So good to meet you! I am Mrs. Andrus." The teacher kindly exclaimed. "How are you feeling? Excited?"

"Oh yes, very much!"

"Glad to hear it. We've been carving pumpkins for the last hour or so, would you like to help? I see Katie and Michael in the corner are having some trouble."

Margaret immediately jumped on the chance, and went over to help the children. The small seat she sat on reminded her of the years when, she too, was a student. The thought of it saddened her. It reminded her of the inevitability that all the children would one day grow up, and never understand the gift of youth until it is lost.

Now it was at about this time, when the oddity that would soon define her life, began to take a very serious and unexpected turn from normality. So mysterious in fact, that it has yet to be understood to this very day. At the moment she reached across the table to pick up a small carving knife, the object miraculously and inexplicably turned to gold at her touch. Astonished by the magic, Margaret remained in utter shock for minutes after. Truly, how could such a thing happen? What possible explanation could there be, and why purely out of the woodwork? Curious, she tried to pick up another, questioning if it too, would do the same.

"If such a miracle as this could happen, why not a second time? It's not beyond the stretch of imagination." She thought.

And as it just so happened, the second did in fact change its composition to a glimmering knife of gold. She stood from her seat, jarred and fascinated by her gift. At the same moment, Ms. Andrus noticed the wonder and cried in enjoyment for the children to watch—of course thinking it no more than a simple magic trick or sleight of hand. When the children became fixated on her, she simply played along with their speculation so as not to alarm them. The incident brought so much adoration, that even after offering candy, Ms. Andrus was unable to get their attention. For the rest of the day, Margaret was fortunate enough to successfully evade touching any more objects (of course to the dismay of the students). The second the final bell rang, she quickly rushed out the door without a goodbye, and ran home without her bike, fearing it too would come under her power and be useless.

On her way home, a friend of her sister's—who was also a fellow gardener—stopped her and asked for assistance in tending to her flowers. Although in a hurry and still in shock from what had befallen her, she simply couldn't deny helping the woman, and generously abided in planting a bushel of Morning Glories. For that was the kind soul Ms. Lincoln was.

The more she volunteered, the more exceedingly difficult the task became. The shovel and rake turned to gold, as did every flower and rock she came into contact with. Soon it was apparent she'd be more detrimental to the woman than of any aid, and so regrettably left, sad that she could not further help. Meanwhile, the lady was extremely elated at the sight of her new golden flowers, and rather than disappointed at Margaret's sudden departure, she felt nothing more than utter gratitude. If she held any disappointment, it was not being able to properly thank her.

When she got home, she locked herself in her room and stayed in bed the remaining day. Without a word or explanation, her mother assumed the worst of her first day, and would worryingly check at her daughter's door throughout the night. It was her interpretation that Margaret lost her job, and likewise felt it best let her sleep the grief off. But as her mother and sister subtly pondered over what could be troubling her, Margaret struggled tens of times over. No longer could she even lay in her bed alone—for that too (as well as her clothes) had turned to gold. And yet, though being gold, such were neither stiff nor hard. The linen which she wore, remained as soft and malleable as ever; simply the appearance had changed. It was as though the gold physically manifested the always-metaphorical grace of linen, and brought to the surface its true, inner beauty, which even the most pessimistic could no longer turn away from.

Once awake, all the previous day's surprises were to culminate in a more unsettling effect. Margaret—who prayed while opening her eyes that the seemingly impossible miracles she knew were nothing more than a dream—found that not only were they very much real, but that now even her skin had turned to gold. When she stood off the bed, the floorboards did the same, as did the door knob, and as did her breakfast toast. Despite complete uncertainty for why this was occurring, and specifically to her, she still felt a deep longing for her ambitions. Not even a detriment of that scale would stand in the way of her dreams. She put on a dress and make up and decided to embrace the golden look as a performance—albeit unorthodox.

Now as hard as it is to believe, upon her mother and sister seeing their home turn to gold before their eyes, they were more happy than bewildered. Perhaps being so desperate for money, they cared more for having it rather than from who and where it came.

"We are going to be rich! Rich Margaret! We will never have to work again!" Her mother shouted with tears of joy.

As she tried to leave, her mother grabbed her and pleaded that she stay.

"Why go to that worthless job? Fate's given us all the money and fame we'll ever need right here! On our very homestead if you can believe it."

But Margaret was fixed to see her children and kindly explained to her mother that she would return later that evening. Eventually she was let to leave and made it to the school, where the students immediately complimented her attire, assuming she had done so in celebration of Halloween. But when some of them went to hug her, their skin turned to gold as well. While the teacher became frantic in the mess, more and more the children wanted a turn, and they surrounded the miss. Not knowing whether to allow them the magic or not and fearing for their safety, she attempted to avoid them. Quickly Mrs. Andrus rushed out of the room and returned with the school officials who—not knowing what to make of the incident—proclaimed that Margaret was a health hazard and fired her not long after.

She left the school for the second time in a state of turmoil. Ms. Lincoln had not known what was becoming of her; but only that it was a terrible curse she could not shake despite how hard she tried. Above all, she was troubled by the old thought. The dream of never succeeding in the world the way she'd always hoped. For as she—one of the few on the island—knew, endless gold could not bring her the happiness she sought. When she arrived home (having now looked more like an elaborate circus than a house), every inch of the drive up and street leading up to it was filled by people eager to get their share. As though the house was an amusement park, and they were obliged to it. Customers and visitors from all corners of the island stood in awe and admiration, buying common household items from the mother, who appointed herself as the cashier.

"Margaret, Margaret, come here! Come take a picture for the newspapers!" Her mother yelled in excitement as dozens of reporters lit up the living room with flashes.

The moment the journalists left, she found herself trapped inside the living room. In front of the doorway spewed a thick line of people—all demanding that she bargain with them and answer questions. Although knowing no way to satisfy them, nor how to provide an explanation, Margaret understood their curiosity and humored them as much as she could.

The first in line, were a series of wealthy bankers who promised to make Margaret a very rich woman if she would join their bank, represent them, and allow them to handle her assets. Not well-versed in financial-talk, she accepted, with the condition that all money given to her instead go to the people who needed it more than herself. The bankers, however, did not want said assets liquidated to the people. They wanted to hold onto all of Margaret's gold. Once they explained this, they were turned down, and stormed out of the room infuriated.

Next, came hundreds of priests from every religion, and from every part of the world. Each one preaching that the lady could surely be nothing less than a divine messenger from their deities, or even God himself. Some bowed before her; others offered elegant gifts. All however, commanded that she return with them and join their followings.

"You can represent us. You can lead our people, you understand?" They each explained in different tongues. "Show humanity the true way, and overrule all the other false ideologies with your special power."

But this power scared Margaret, and she would neither lead people she had never known, nor attempt to undermine those who disagreed with her.

When the endless sects of religious leaders saw Margaret was not to join their various factions, many spit at her golden feet and left angrily.

"You are a false preacher then! A false teacher and omen!" They obnoxiously declared, upon being rejected by the miss.

After, came the scientists, who wished to take Margaret for themselves in order to experiment on.

"She is most certainly not a god or messenger." They arrogantly explained to others in line. "All can be explained through science, and this woman of precious metal is nothing more than a charlatan. The gold is either an illusion, or a rare scientific phenomenon yet to be understood. We will find out, and provide answers for the people. We are the voices of reason, and the interested citizens should consult us, rather than her or other groups."

To these people, she also declined.

"I am sorry. Though I wish to help you, I do not wish to be experimented on, and know full-well that this matter is beyond empirical science." She calmly explained. But they, too, scoffed at her.

Then came an older woman. Dressed ornately in fancy robes and jewels. She explained helplessly to Margaret that her children are ill and in need of financial assistance. She went on, that she was in fact very poor, and only had those clothes to sell off. When Margaret rationalized that were she to give gold to the woman, she would have to turn everything into gold for all who desired it. She insisted that the woman rather sell her lofty attire and use the money from that. The woman had none of it, and conceitedly ridiculed Margaret. She proceeded to slap her across the face, and walked away, stomping her feet. Not one in the room batted an eye.

Upset and with no direction to turn, Margaret closed the door to the house as her mother continued to entertain the crowd outside. She watched the news on television, which showed people all over the globe discussing her and the home. Word spread fast, as did those whose profession was to exploit others. She saw her information flash across the screen on every channel. Past friends of hers were interviewed. They explained her favorite foods, shows, activities, the type of bike she rode—even her address and phone numbers so openly. Many reporters were skeptical of her abilities. But some out of these there were in the crowd, who went to see for themselves and became true believers. The channels differed significantly in their portrayal of her. Some supported Margaret, and claimed she was a hidden queen amongst mankind. Others pronounced these people as buffoons, and said she was but a fraud tricking the people. Some lied and said she obtained her gold through stealing from the poor and melting the metal down, while others described how she always gave her gold to the impoverished. Over and over, they obsessed over the miss and her quaint home. The more unbelievable they could spin the story, the unbelievably more people tuned in.

With every passing hour, the eye's of the people widened, and the size of the crowd expanded. Soon the herd could not be tamed. The people, frenzied by the illusion of wealth, and angered by the selfishness of Margaret, broke through the windows. They wanted the golden objects of the Lincoln home, and they wanted the Golden Lady.

"Turn our objects into gold!" They demanded. "We deserve it! We will use it for the good!"

Equally curious to Margaret's powers, was what happened when the greedy people touched an object of gold. Immediately upon placing their fingers to it, their objects returned to their original state and lost all their glint. When, for instance, the Golden Lady transformed a lampshade for a man, it became the raggedy lamp it'd always been once placed back into his hands. This was interestingly not the case with children. For they could freely handle the gold and keep it for themselves. A number of adults were an exception as well, though remarkably rare. These people then—once having caught the attention of the people—soon became targets of raid and robbery.

Margaret ran out her backdoor to flee, while the mob chased quickly behind. She ran across the city attempting to hide, but for every building that turned to gold, the people knew where she lurked. And by the early evening, a spectacular scene, one just as incredible as Margaret herself, was beginning to take place on Harrington Island. An entire city of brilliant yellow sparked through the salty air. Nearly every building, house, plant, animal, and child, had turned to gold and spread like a virus. All The While, the angered crowd of people tore through the city, reverting the miracle step-by-step.

The mob—which in every sense of the word, the people became—slowly began to turn into a revolt against Margaret. The greed and optimism they once shared together, was swiftly deteriorating into a blood-laden pool of rage and hysteria, from which any sense of consequence had been thrown away with the thought of infinite power and gold. They were crazed by poisonous thoughts, obsessed with the thought of such power and potential. They dreamt as they marched: the dark dreams of narrow-minded dreamers. They dreamed of the possibilities—to become rulers, to become the self-proclaimed enlightened ones, who by virtue of their illustrious possessions Fate had endowed them with sovereign authority. They were not to be stopped.

Eventually, Margaret got to the school which had still been untouched by the crowds. In it, huddled closely into the corner of two bookshelves, were her students who had turned to gold, frightened and sad. Presumably, they were left there the past day by the school staff, for fear of contamination. Their assistant teacher sat beside them and comforted them that they would not be found. Yet, by the nature and mentality that is a crazed group bent on revolt without reason, they were in fact found, and the locked door flew to the ground. They wanted the gold for themselves, and not being able to touch it while mere children could, infuriated them even more. Some were so desperate, they momentarily calmed the flames in their eyes to gently sit beside the children and offer to be their parents.

They grabbed Margaret and the children and brought them to the top of the city's highest building. They tied the Golden Lady to a pole and demanded she turn them without reverting back. Despite explaining to them the power was out of her control, and that she could not meet their commands even if she wanted to, the people were unrelenting and tortured her.

"I cannot turn you into gold, don't you understand?".

"Turn us! Turn us! Turn our possessions!" They cried. "Stop lying and turn us!"

"I cannot." She explained, weeping. "Why must you be literal gold? Can you not present yourselves as golden, see things as though they were gold, and be equally happy?"

"But why must we be children? Why aren't we allowed to have your gift?" One shouted.

"Perhaps because you must ask that; because you've lost all hope in the possibility of having it by your own motivation. My dream was to help you—it grew so much that it couldn't be contained within me and leaked into the world. You've all suppressed your dreams and let them become so small within you, that you need ours; you need it for compensation. You need those whose dreams have not died, so that things in your world can still become golden. Why must your dreams be only the faith in the dreams of others?"

But as passionate and well-versed as the Golden Lady was, not one listened. The disgusting men and women surrounded her in perpetual yelling and assaults. They were sure of nothing, but that she was lying. And indeed, when one has set their mind on such a strong conviction, there is no reasoning on Earth to persuade them otherwise. Around the pole were filthy faces smeared with dirt and soot. Their hair blackened, eyes reddened, and mouths shouted as maggots fell from rotting teeth. And at that moment, for the first time, Margaret did not regret what came of her. For if turning to gold made her in any way different from all those ugly beasts who cursed foul words at her, then she was very thankful, and would rather be in no other position than that of the one tied to the pole.

It could've been possible for the mob to stop and return to their homes. It could've been possible. But as the events were to unfold, and by the title of the headlines for the following day's local newspapers regarding the incident—what would sadly come next of our Margaret Lincoln would be none other than that of a tragedy.

After terrible actions performed as a last effort for gold (which I will leave open for the reader's interpretation), the pole was thrown off the building at the stroke of midnight. It was the only light which lit the city as it fell. Instantly, once the light went out, everything that had been turned went back to its original state. What remained was a normal city left in ruin. That is, except for the children and the few adults who had been turned to gold. Oddly enough, they remained—for the specific gold they wore did not leave with Margaret.

The revolt calmed, and the people watched as the splendor they lusted for so highly, evaporated before their eyes and by their dirty hands. They quietly thought throughout the remaining night how to deal with those still affected with the magic. They too could be tied up and forced to reveal their secrets, but as the Golden Miss showed, it would be fruitless. It was unanimously decided by the people, that a large ship from one of the ports would be fitted heftily with supplies, and the golden ones would be sent away from the island. They could be of no use, and would only torture the people with untouchable envy. The special ones were seen as a curse, and from that point onward, the revolt was declared their fault. Although, within it—however small and unspoken—did come a new sense of realization in the minds of the mob. That just as easily can people of innocence be turned into gold, so could they be tainted by the filth of greed. And once something as horrid as greed infects a one as vigorously as it does, there is little one can do to cure himself of it. Perhaps then, their subconscious celebrated the children's futures.

When the next morning came, the special ones sat aboard their golden ship and dreamt of where it would sail. On the shore of the island, the people stood and watched as they departed—looking down in remorse, and knowing they would never be as rich as the children or that of Margaret Lincoln.

~END~